COQUÍ IN THE CITY

NOMAR PEREZ

Dial Books for Young Readers

In San Juan, Miguel brought his pet frog, Coquí, everywhere.

He brought him to play baseball with his friends,

to visit the pond
in the park,

and to buy quesitos,
his favorite snack,
from the panadería.

Coquí was part of the familia. Miguel brought him to every dinner at his abuelos' house. Coquí even seemed to listen to the family as they laughed and told stories.

"Abuelo! Tell me the story about when you met Roberto Clemente!" Miguel said, even though he'd heard the story a hundred times already. Miguel's abuelo loved baseball just as much as he did.

At home, Miguel snuggled in bed as the sounds of the night covered him like a warm blanket. Coquí and his friends sang him to sleep.

COQUÍ
COQUÍ

One morning, Mamá and Papá had some important news.
"Nos vamos pa' alla afuera, hijo."
They were moving to the United States mainland.

"Will there be baseball there?" Miguel asked.
"Definitely," said Papá.
"And quesitos?"
"I'm not sure, but we will find out!" Mamá answered.

Miguel started to pack up his life in Puerto Rico, but his mind wandered to all the things he would miss:

flying kites en el Morro,

going to his abuelos' house, and climbing the mango tree in the backyard,

and playing a güiro in a parranda with family and friends during la Navidad.

But most of all, Miguel would miss Coquí.
"I wish I could bring you along," he whispered to Coquí at the airport.
"Coquí, coquí," his friend replied.

"Adios, Coquí," Miguel said, and placed Coquí in the gentle hands of his abuelo.

"Don't worry, Miguelito, everything is going to be all right," Abuelo assured Miguel.

"La canción del Coquí will be with you everywhere you go. Coquí will be in your smile, in your warm hugs, in your new adventures, and most importantly in your loving heart," Abuelo said, pulling from his pocket a little surprise.

It was an old baseball signed by the baseball legend
Roberto Clemente!

"Wow, for me?" Miguel asked.

"Sí," Abuelo smiled. "To keep you company everywhere you go."

Miguel fell asleep on the airplane, holding the baseball tightly.
"Mira, mijo. Look!" Mamá said, shaking him awake.
Down below, hundreds of bright lights twinkled.
"Look how tall the buildings are!"

When they arrived at the apartment, Miguel couldn't believe how much smaller it was than their house back in San Juan.

As they unpacked in their new home, Miguel said, "Mamá, I miss Coquí."

"I know, mijo, and I miss Abuelo and Abuela too," Mamá said softly.
"Yes, I miss their hugs," Miguel said.
"Why don't we go outside and explore the neighborhood before
Papá comes back from work? That'll take our minds off of everything."

The streets were full of interesting sights, sounds, and people.
Spanish words danced around them, and other unfamiliar languages too.
The newness of everything was overwhelming.

JACOB'S SHOE REPAIR

Sabor

ASIA MARKET

BARBER SHOP

SALE

PRETZELS

Then, Miguel and Mamá happened upon something familiar—
a park!

"Mira Mamá, tienen empanadillas," said Miguel, excited to
see something else he recognized.

But as they were walking toward the fritura vendor,
an interesting sound caught Miguel's attention.

Croac
Croac

ribbit
ribbit

"Coquí?" Miguel said, looking around him.

He found a small pond, full of frogs, hopping, splashing, and catching flies on their tongues just like his Coquí. "Mamá, mira! Can I take one home?" Miguel asked.

Mamá laughed. "No, mijo, let's keep exploring."

When they stumbled onto a baseball field near the pond, Mamá said, "Let's play some catch!"

Miguel still missed home, but throwing his Roberto Clemente baseball made him feel a little bit better.

After the game, Miguel and Mamá started home. They spotted a panadería, just like the ones back in Puerto Rico. And guess who was standing there with a box of quesitos in his hand? Papá!

At home, the sun was slowly dropping down behind the buildings while Miguel and his parents ate together. They were tired from the day, but it was a good kind of tired.

ENJOY

ARTE

Miguel snuggled in bed as the sounds of the city at night covered him like a warm blanket. Soft Spanish music drifted in from his neighbor's window. Miguel whispered a quiet *coquí, coquí* to himself and thought about his Coquí and all of the people and places he loved in Puerto Rico. They would always be close to his heart, no matter where he was. Some things were definitely different in New York, but some things were just the same.

To my wife, Farah, for her constant support and love.

To my kids, Nathanael, Jacob, and Aliah, for their inspiration.

To my parents, Papito y Mamita, who sacrificed their all
to move six kids to the U.S.

To all Puerto Ricans living in and out of the island,
may we continue to make our mark in this world.

Dial Books for Young Readers
An imprint of Penguin Random House LLC, New York

First published in the United States of America by Dial Books for Young Readers,
an imprint of Penguin Random House LLC, 2021

Visit us online at penguinrandomhouse.com.

Library of Congress Cataloging-in-Publication Data

Names: Perez, Nomar, date, author, illustrator.
Title: Coquí in the city / Nomar Perez.
Description: New York : Dial Books for Young Readers, 2021. | Audience:
  Ages 3–7. | Audience: Grades K–1 | Summary: "When Miguel and his parents move from
  Puerto Rico to the U.S. mainland, Miguel misses their home, his grandparents, and his
  pet frog, Coquí, but he soon realizes that New York City has more in common with back
  home than he originally thought"—Provided by publisher.
Identifiers: LCCN 2020027820 (print) | LCCN 2020027821 (ebook) | ISBN 9780593109038 (hardcover)
  ISBN 9780593109045 (ebook) | ISBN 9780593109052 (kindle edition)
Subjects: CYAC: Moving, Household—Fiction. | Puerto Ricans—New York
  (State) New York—Fiction. | Frogs—Fiction. | New York (N.Y.)—Fiction.
Classification: LCC PZ7.1.P44749 Co 2021 (print) | LCC PZ7.1.P44749 (ebook) | DDC [E]—dc23
LC record available at https://lccn.loc.gov/2020027820
LC ebook record available at https://lccn.loc.gov/2020027821
Manufactured in China
ISBN 9780593109038

10 9 8 7 6 5 4 3 2 1

Design by Mina Chung • Text set in Caecilia Com